Teacher's Pet

MARGUERITE HENRY'S Misty Inn

Teacher's Pet

By Judy Katschke

Illustrated by Serena Geddes

ALADDIN

New York London Toronto Sydney New Delhi

ALADDIN

An imprint of Simon & Schuster Children's Publishing Division

1230 Avenue of the Americas, New York, New York 10020

First Aladdin paperback edition July 2017

Text copyright © 2017 by The Estate of Marguerite Henry

Illustrations copyright © 2017 by Serena Geddes

Also available in an Aladdin hardcover edition.

All rights reserved, including the right of reproduction in whole or in part in any form.

ALADDIN and related logo are registered trademarks of Simon & Schuster, Inc.

For information about special discounts for bulk purchases, please contact Simon & Schuster Special Sales at 1-866-506-1949 or business@simonandschuster.com.

The Simon & Schuster Speakers Bureau can bring authors to your live event. For more information or to book an event contact the Simon & Schuster Speakers Bureau at 1-866-248-3049 or visit our website at www.simonspeakers.com.

Book designed by Laura Lyn DiSiena

The text of this book was set in Century Expanded.

Manufactured in the United States of America 1219 OFF

10 9 8 7 6 5

Library of Congress Control Number 2016962811

ISBN 978-1-4814-6992-0 (hc)

ISBN 978-1-4814-6991-3 (pbk)

ISBN 978-1-4814-6993-7 (eBook)

For Susan

Teacher's Pet

Chapter 1

"WHAT DO YOU THINK OF THIS IDEA?" WILLA Dunlap asked her best friends as they climbed aboard the school bus. "A how-to speech—on how to give a how-to speech!"

Sarah Starling and Lena Wise smiled along with Willa as they scrambled for empty seats. They didn't usually talk about homework on the ride home. But this assignment was unusual!

"Remember," Sarah called across the aisle to Willa and Lena. "Ms. Denise said our how-to speeches should say something about ourselves."

"Like what?" Lena asked.

Willa had a suggestion. "You love solving mysteries, Lena," she said. "Maybe you can find something that went missing in the classroom."

"First you'd have to make something disappear," Sarah said. "What could it be?"

Lena rolled her eyes. "How about this homework?" she joked.

Willa giggled. Ms. Denise's assignment couldn't be *that* bad!

"We practically have two weeks to put our how-to speeches together," Willa said as she pulled out her notebook. On the cover was a picture of a butterscotch-colored pony grazing in a green pasture. To Willa, the horse looked just like her own buckskin mare, Starbuck. If she couldn't bring Starbuck to school, her notebook was the next best thing!

"First we have to pick a topic," Willa stated as she looked over her notes. "Next we have to write an outline of important points."

Willa smiled at that part. Ms. Denise had explained that an outline was like a list of ideas. And Willa loved making lists!

"Last but not least," Willa went on, "we write our introduction and conclusion with a how-to speech in between."

"Somebody save me a seat by the window!" someone called out. Willa looked up to see Olivia Bradley hurrying up the aisle of the bus. Olivia and her family had just moved to Chincoteague Island from New York. She sometimes had a way of walking that reminded Willa of a prancing pony.

After Olivia brushed by, Willa shut her notebook.

"The hardest part of this how-to demo," Willa told Sarah and Lena, "is figuring out the how-to."

Mr. Carmichael, the school bus operator, took a head count. When he was done, he shouted, "What are we waiting for? Let's get this big yellow stagecoach on the trail!"

Riding the bus was fun with Mr. Carmichael at the wheel. Today he was a stagecoach driver, but just yesterday he was an astronaut manning a spaceship. How had Willa walked to school and back every day when she lived in Chicago?

The bus became noisy with chatter as it pulled away from the school. But Willa, Sarah, and Lena sat in silence thinking about their how-to speeches.

"Maybe I can do a how-to speech on how to clean the hamster cage," Lena said.

"Then you'd have to clean the hamster cage," Willa pointed out.

Lena wrinkled her nose. "Forget that idea."

Willa gazed out the window. It was the middle of September. Most of the trees were still green with speckles of red and gold beginning to appear.

Just then Willa noticed they were passing Ms. Denise, who was riding her bike. The school year had just started, but so far Ms. Denise seemed to be a good teacher, with a cool sense of humor. She kept bobblehead dolls of Lincoln and Washington on her desk and wore the same color almost every day—bright pinkish red. Even her bike was that color!

Bike . . . hmm.

"Maybe," Willa said, "I could do a demonstration on how to ride a bike."

"This is Chincoteague Island, Willa," Sarah

said politely. "Practically all the kids here already know how to ride bikes."

"Right." Willa sighed. She sometimes had to remind herself she was no longer in Chicago. Not all kids rode bikes in the big city.

"Hey!" Sarah cried as a crunched-up ball of paper bounced off her head. Spinning around, Willa spotted the culprits: her little brother, Ben, and Sarah's little brother, Chipper Starling, laughing it up a few seats back.

Sarah groaned as she slumped back in her seat. "I think I just came up with the best how-to topic ever," she muttered.

"What?" Willa asked.

"How to get our pesty little brothers grounded for life!" Sarah declared.

By the time Willa stepped off the bus with Ben, she had forgotten all about the flying spitball. She was still busy thinking about Ms. Denise's how-to speech. What would she talk about?

A how-to speech on folding sweaters in your drawer? Willa thought. *The fastest way to clean your room? How to squeeze toothpaste out of the tube so you don't waste a drop?*

Ben had no trouble knowing what to talk about as they walked up the short hill from the road to their house. . . .

"Lawrence threw up during recess all over Shelby's new sneakers," Ben rambled. "We had a substitute teacher today with purple streaks in her hair and her name was Ms. Lavender. I'm not kidding, Willa. That was her real name!"

"Uh-huh," Willa said, not really hearing.

She and Ben turned onto the path leading to the big Victorian house they called home. It was also called Misty Inn, ever since their parents turned it into a working bed-and-breakfast.

Willa's dad had worked as a chef in Chicago. Now he was happy to cook for the inn's restaurant, the Family Farm.

But for Willa, the best part about moving

from Chicago to Chincoteague Island was the four-legged animal grazing in the pasture a few feet away. . . .

"Hi, Starbuck!" Willa called happily.

The butterscotch-colored mare lifted her head. Shaking her shaggy black mane, she nickered at the sight of Willa and Ben. But as Willa got a better look at Starbuck, she frowned.

"Somebody was rolling in the mud again." Willa sighed. She placed her backpack on the ground to flick a flake of mud from Starbuck's forehead. The mud had practically covered the pretty white star that inspired her name.

"I thought only dogs rolled in the mud," Ben said.

"Sometimes horses roll to dry off their sweat," Willa explained. "Also, mud and dirt make good insect repellents. Horses know that."

"How do you know so much about ponies and mud?" Ben asked.

"Grandma Edna," Willa said as she dusted off Starbuck's mane with a gentle hand. "How else?"

Willa and Ben's grandmother was a veterinarian on Chincoteague Island. Not only did she run an animal-care center on her own farm, she'd taught Willa everything she knew about caring for Starbuck.

"This is the third time this week Starbuck got so muddy," Willa said. "I don't get it."

"I'm sure Starbuck doesn't mind," Ben said. "She's a wild pony, remember?"

"How can I forget?" Willa smiled. She was the proud owner of an honest-to-goodness Chincoteague pony.

Every summer, in the last week of July, a herd of wild ponies would swim from nearby Assateague Island to Chincoteague. The ponies were skillfully led by "saltwater cowboys," volunteer firemen who ran the famous event. Shortly after the pony swim, something just as exciting would come—the pony auction. That's where people from all over the world would bid for their own Chincoteague pony.

Willa didn't have to bid for Starbuck. After being cared for at Grandma Edna's rescue center, the determined pony walked all the way from Miller Farm to her new home—Misty Inn!

"Can you take my backpack into the house, please?" Willa asked Ben. "I want to take Starbuck into the barn to groom her."

"Before your after-school snack?" Ben asked.

"Dad said he might try out a new chocolate chip cookie recipe today."

Willa shook her head as she took hold of Starbuck's halter. "A dirty pony right outside the inn can't be good for business," she said.

Willa was about to steer Starbuck toward the barn when the sweet smell of something yummy drifted through the air.

"Mmm," Willa said taking a whiff. "Do you smell that?"

Ben grinned. "It doesn't smell like chocolate chip cookies, and it sure doesn't smell like a dirty pony."

Willa turned her pony toward the barn. Whatever that aroma coming from the kitchen was—grooming Starbuck would have to wait!

Chapter 2

THE MYSTERY OF THE DELICIOUS SMELL WAS solved the moment Willa and Ben entered the kitchen.

"Zucchini bread!" Willa exclaimed.

"Is that what's for dinner, Dad?" Ben asked.

"It's for dessert," Dad said as he covered the warm bread with a red-and-white-checkered tea towel. "I've got to find some way to get you guys to eat your veggies."

The zucchini bread wasn't alone on the big butcher-block table. There was also a huge bowl filled with colorful fruit salad, tomatoes stuffed with couscous and raisins, and what looked like a broccoli-and-cheddar quiche.

Willa gazed at the kitchen counter. On it were baskets filled with Granny Smith apples and purple plums, plus a brown paper bag dotted with red juice-like stains.

"I don't get it, Dad," Willa said. "The Family Farm is closed on Mondays after the summer, so why the cooking spree?"

"I've decided to team up with local Chincoteague farmers," Dad explained, "and serve meals prepared with their produce."

"And here's some more, Eric!" someone boomed.

Willa turned to see a tall man with a grizzled beard walk through the kitchen door. He wore a tie-dyed T-shirt under overalls,

and he was carrying a big basket of corn.

"Willa, Ben, meet Randy Beardan," Dad said.

Beardan . . . beard? Willa thought that was funny.

"Are you a farmer?" Ben asked, nodding at the corn.

"You bet, Ben," Randy replied. "I run the Germination and Meditation Farm, a few miles from here."

"Germination . . . and Meditation?" Willa repeated.

"'Germination' is a farming term," Randy explained as he placed the basket on the counter with a *THUNK*. "It's when a seedling cracks through the casing and begins to sprout."

Randy turned away from the counter and

said, "The Meditation part is for my wife's Farm and Flex yoga classes."

Mom walked into the kitchen with a smile. "I've gone to Ellen's yoga class, Randy," she said, "and I never knew twisting like a pretzel could be so relaxing."

Willa watched Mom place a few colorful squares of material on the kitchen counter. She was about to ask what they were when Ben pointed to the juice-stained bag.

"I think I know what's inside," Ben said. "Strawberries."

"Excellent guess, Ben," Randy said. "But strawberries aren't in season, so I brought by a freshly grown batch of raspberries."

Farmer Randy pulled a raspberry from the brown bag. Carefully grasping it between his thumb and index finger, he held it up to the window.

"*Rubus idaeus*," Randy announced lovingly. "A hollow core surrounded by multiple fleshy drupelets. When Mother Nature made this beauty, she didn't just grow a fruit—she created a masterpiece!"

Wow, Willa thought. *I'll bet Farmer Randy would give a great how-to speech for Ms. Denise.*

"Okay!" Randy boomed, spinning around to face Willa and Ben. "Who wants to try one of these little gems? Ben? How about you?"

"Um . . . no, thanks." Ben hesitated. "The last raspberry I ate was kind of sour."

"Sour is for lemons, Ben," Randy said gruffly, blinking his eyes. "I prefer the word 'tart.' But the raspberries from my latest crop are far from it."

Willa didn't want Farmer Randy's feelings to be hurt, so she held out her hand and said, "I'll try one, please."

Farmer Randy dropped the raspberry into Willa's palm. "Go for it, Willa," he said. "The taste from this little winner was born to be wild."

Willa popped the raspberry into her mouth. As it slowly dissolved on her tongue, a burst of sugary-sweet flavor exploded in her mouth!

"Oh my gosh, that's awesome!" Willa said. She had finished the raspberry, but the sweet juices were still in her mouth. "This isn't a raspberry—it's a superberry!"

"Me too, please," Ben said, jutting out his palm.

"Knock yourself out!" Farmer Randy said, handing over a raspberry.

Still a bit wary, Ben placed it on his tongue and closed his mouth. A few seconds later he was grinning too.

"Sweet!" Ben declared.

Mom and Dad tried some too, with the same reactions. Farmer Randy's sweet red raspberries were a hit.

"I think I'll bake a special torte just for these raspberries," Dad announced. "And I have just the recipe."

"I didn't know you had a recipe for raspberry torte, Eric," Mom said.

"I don't yet," Dad said. "But my friend Lance in Chicago has a fabulous one I'm sure he'll e-mail me." Dad tilted his head thoughtfully as he smiled at Randy. "Come to think of it . . . I'll name the dessert after the farm the raspberries came from."

"Germination and Meditation?" Willa blurted. She didn't want to be rude, but she couldn't think of a worse name for such a yummy dessert. "I don't think so, Dad."

Willa tapped her chin thoughtfully. She stopped after the fourth tap and smiled. "How about Randy's Razzle-Dazzle Raspberry Torte!"

Randy stroked his beard. "I like it," he said. "You're great at coming up with ideas, Willa Dunlap."

"Thanks," Willa said, enjoying the compliment. "I just have one question. Can horses eat raspberries too?"

"They can, but in moderation," Randy replied. "One or two will do."

Dad and Randy stepped to the side to work out their next order. Willa could see Mom slipping the squares of material into a kitchen drawer.

"What are those, Mom?" Willa asked.

"They're swatches for new dining-room curtains," Mom replied. "Ever since your dad began cooking formal and high-endy meals for the restaurant, I thought I'd do some redecorating."

Redecorating? Willa loved Misty Inn just the way it was, with its antique furniture, floral wallpaper, and comfy sofas and chairs.

"I'm not totally sure yet," Mom went on, "but midcentury modern is trendy right now."

"Misty Inn is midcentury, Mom," Willa

said. "Mid-eighteen hundreds, right?"

"Right," Mom said as she shut the drawer. "Anyway, it's just a little thought I had."

Willa and Ben traded glances. Mom's little thoughts often led to big thoughts, and bigger projects.

"Oh, and one more thing," Mom said as the inn's resident feline, New Cat, circled her legs. "Once we redecorate, New Cat and Amos will have to stay outside."

"Aww, Mom!" Ben complained.

New Cat and Amos the dog were their pets—and important residents of Misty Inn. But Willa didn't have time to worry about Mom's latest project. She had her own project to worry about—Ms. Denise's how-to speech!

♥

Opening the double barn doors, Willa heard a snort of greeting from Starbuck's stall. She was about to close both doors when Amos scampered inside.

"Mom says you might have to stay outside the house, Amos," Willa informed the fluffy little dog. "But you like the barn better, don't you, boy?"

Amos wagged his tail, then scampered back outside to chase a rabbit. Smiling, Willa walked over the hard-packed hay floor to Starbuck's stall.

"I spy with my little eye a muddy pony," Willa said.

Leaning over the door of the stall, she inspected Starbuck's coat. The mud had started to dry, which was good news. Dry mud was way easier to clean off than wet.

Willa usually gave Starbuck a treat after she finished grooming, but this time she couldn't wait. . . .

"These berries are going to sweeten your life, Starbuck," Willa said, pulling a small plastic snack bag from her pocket. She held out two almost-squished raspberries in her hand, her

palm flat. Starbuck nibbled one, then gobbled the other.

"Dad is getting a recipe just for these raspberries," Willa said. "I named it Randy's Razzle-Dazzle Raspberry Torte."

Starbuck nudged Willa's fist for more. Willa opened her hand to show it was empty.

"Farmer Randy said I'm great at coming up with ideas," Willa said as she collected an armful of grooming tools. "Now if I can just come up with an idea for Ms. Denise's how-to speech!"

Chapter 3

"*A* IS FOR APRICOT," WILLA SANG AS SHE jumped up and down. "*B* is for bird—"

Going through the alphabet helped her parents remember things—so maybe it would help Willa and her friends come up with an idea for their assignment.

"I know! I know!" Sarah shouted as she

turned the jump rope. "A how-to speech on how to build a bird feeder."

Lena shook her head as she turned the other side of the rope. "Ms. Denise will never let us use sharp tools in the classroom," she called out.

Willa continued jumping. "*C* is for candy, *D* is for dinosaur . . ."

Sarah shouted again, "A how-to speech on

different dinosaurs in prehistoric times. We can make them out of clay—"

"We did that in kindergarten," Lena cut in.

Willa stopped jumping, and the other girls let the rope drop. It was Wednesday, and the three friends still had no topic for their how-to speeches.

On the bus that morning Willa, Sarah, and Lena had decided to team up for the how-to speech. Ms. Denise said they could as long as teams were no bigger than three kids. There was one problem: coming up with a team idea was just as hard as coming up with a solo idea!

"We have two days to tell Ms. Denise our ideas, today and tomorrow," Willa reminded. "If birdhouses and dinosaurs aren't good ones, what are?"

"I don't know," Lena admitted. "Ms. Denise said these how-to speeches should be like getting-to-know-you speeches. So we have to tell the others about ourselves."

"But everyone already knows one another!" Sarah said.

"Almost everybody," Willa reminded. "Olivia Bradley just moved to Chincoteague two weeks ago. She's even newer than I am."

Willa, Sarah, and Lena spotted Olivia standing alone at the water fountain.

"We should go over and say hi," Willa suggested.

"We don't have to," Lena said. "Here she comes."

Olivia had begun walking over, stepping high again like a prancing horse. Something was coiled up in one of her hands. As Olivia got closer, Willa saw it was a jump rope.

"I saw you guys jumping rope," Olivia said.

"Do you want to jump with us?" Willa asked with a smile.

"No, thanks," Olivia said. She held up her hand and let the jump rope uncoil straight to the ground. "Not until I show you how it's *really* done."

"*Really* done?" Sarah asked, confused.

"What's wrong with the way we jump rope?" Lena asked.

"It's not the way you jump rope, it's how you jump rope," Olivia explained. "In my old neighborhood a lot of us jumped with two ropes."

"You mean double Dutch?" Willa asked. "Some kids in my Chicago school jumped rope that way. It's pretty awesome."

"Know what's even more awesome?" Olivia asked. "Winning third prize in the Double Dutch Challenge this summer."

"You won a contest?" Sarah gasped, impressed. "Could you show us how to jump double Dutch?"

"For sure," Olivia said. "And after you guys learn the ropes, we can give a how-to speech for Ms. Denise."

Willa, Sarah, and Lena traded confused looks. Since when had they agreed to do their how-to speech on double Dutch?

"Um . . . Olivia?" Willa asked. "Did you just say a how-to speech?"

"On double Dutch," Olivia said with a nod. "All it takes is a little practice."

"But—" Lena started to say.

"We have a few minutes before the bell rings," Olivia cut in. "So let's start with turning the rope. . . . You and you."

Olivia pointed to Lena and Sarah. The two friends shrugged, then both said, "Okay."

Willa didn't mind that they were the rope turners. *I'll probably get to jump in*, she thought.

Willa watched as Olivia showed Sarah and Lena how to hold both handles while turning two ropes.

"When one hand is up the other is down," Olivia directed. "Remember to hold the ropes high and turn them in the opposite directions."

To get the beat, Olivia began to rhyme: "Berries, berries on a dish—how many berries do you wish?"

After a few goof ups, Lena and Sarah found their rhythm. Soon they were spinning both ropes double Dutch!

"Should I jump in now, Olivia?" Willa asked.

"Nope," Olivia said. She jumped sideways into the turning ropes. Once in she began jumping back and forth over the ropes, even spinning and jumping on one foot.

Olivia's feet moved so fast they were a blur. *No wonder she walks like a prancing horse,* Willa decided.

Other kids crowded around to watch the double Dutchers. Some were tapping their feet to the beat or trying to jump up and down like Olivia.

The ropes became tangled and Olivia stumbled.

"Can I try?" a second grader called out.

"Me, me!" a boy from first grade piped up.

Olivia shook her head and said, "Maybe another time."

As the disappointed kids walked away, Olivia smiled at Sarah and Lena. "You're pretty good for newbies," she said. "All you have to do is practice enough for our how-to speech."

"Cool!" Lena said with a smile.

"We'll be great!" Sarah insisted happily.

But to Willa something didn't seem right.

"Olivia, if Lena and Sarah are turning the ropes and you're jumping," Willa asked. "What would I be doing?"

With a shrug Olivia said, "Ms. Denise said we can only have three to a team. So . . . sorry, Willa."

Willa's heart sank until Lena spoke up.

"Sorry too, Olivia," Lena said, shaking her head. "We won't do it without Willa."

"We were going to team up the three of us," Sarah explained, "as soon as we figured out a how-to topic."

"So you won't do it?" Olivia asked.

Deep inside, Willa didn't want her friends to do a how-to speech without her. But she also didn't want to keep them from having fun. So—

"Go ahead," Willa blurted. "I'm okay if you do it without me."

Lena and Sarah stared at Willa.

"Are you sure?" Lena asked.

"Really okay?" Sarah asked.

Willa was almost ready to cry out, but she nodded, then forced herself to say, "I'll just do my own how-to speech. It's okay . . . really."

"Awesome," Olivia said as the bell rang. "I'll return the jump ropes and meet you guys inside."

Willa walked quietly with Sarah and Lena across the schoolyard toward the door. *Should I have told Sarah and Lena the truth?* she wondered. *That I don't want them to do a how-to speech without me?*

But as they walked inside, Willa had a hopeful thought:

They won't do it. They know we're a team!

"I hope everyone had a fun recess," Ms. Denise said, writing the words "How-to Speeches" on the board. "Before we go over last night's math homework, I want to hear some of your how-to ideas."

Excited whispers filled the room. Willa

wished she had a how-to speech idea, but she wasn't even sure she had a how-to team.

"Okay!" Ms. Denise said, facing the class. She was wearing a cardigan in her favorite pink color, which matched her lipstick. "Who wants to go first?"

Jasper Langely's hand shot in the air. "I do, Ms. Denise!"

"Go ahead, Jasper," Ms. Denise said. She turned to the board ready to write his idea.

"I want to show the class how to burp the alphabet," Jasper explained. "First I drink a huge bottle of soda. Then I wait a few minutes for the gas to build up. Then I let 'er rip!"

Laughter and groans filled the classroom. Willa rolled her eyes. What did they expect from Jasper?

"Drinking a whole gallon of soda can't be healthy, Jasper," Ms. Denise said.

Jasper was silent, then piped up, "Then I'll drink a half gallon and only burp from *A* to *J*!"

Ms. Denise seemed to take a deep breath. "Burping isn't appropriate for this project," she said. "Please rethink your how-to speech, Jasper."

"Okay." He sighed.

"Anybody else?" Ms. Denise asked.

The next hand to go up was Melanie Pendergast's. Melanie lived in the biggest house on Chincoteague Island. Her barn held four Chincoteague ponies!

"Go ahead, Melanie," Ms. Denise said.

Turning around to face the class, Melanie said, "I'd like to do a how-to speech on making a family tree. The branches of your family tree show all your relatives that came before you."

"A family tree," Ms. Denise said as she wrote the words on the board. "That's a good how-to idea, Melanie."

"Thank you, Ms. Denise," Melanie answered. "I already started researching my family history, and I'm pretty sure I'll find a king or a queen."

"Or a princess," Jasper scoffed.

Ms. Denise pointed a warning finger at Jasper, then continued. "I know I'll hear some more great ideas today," she said. "Anyone?"

"I'd like to do a how-to speech on how to jump rope double Dutch, Ms. Denise," Olivia called out from the back of the classroom. "That's jumping with two jump ropes."

"That sounds interesting, Olivia," Ms. Denise

admitted. "But wouldn't you need others to jump with you?"

"I already have," Olivia said. "Sarah and Lena."

Ms. Denise's eyes found Lena in the first row, and Sarah sitting behind Willa. "Are you both teaming up with Olivia, girls?" she asked.

Willa held her breath. *They'll say no. For sure.*

After a few seconds Lena spoke. . . . "Yes, Ms. Denise," she said.

Then Sarah: "I am too, Ms. Denise."

What? Willa stared ahead at Lena. She then spun around to stare at Sarah.

"What, Willa?" Sarah whispered. "You said it was okay. Doubly-triply!"

Willa faced forward. She knew what she'd said, but it wasn't okay. Not really. She still didn't have a how-to speech. And now her best friends were doing one—without her!

Chapter 4

"WEREN'T YOU SUPPOSED TO GET TOGETHER with Sarah and Lena this afternoon," Dad asked Willa, "to talk about your how-to speeches?"

Mr. Dunlap was preparing dinner, expertly slicing a crisp, red pepper. Willa sat on a high stool at the kitchen table, snacking on the last of the red raspberries. Ben was over at the Starlings', so she tried to leave a few for him. It wasn't easy.

"Sarah and Lena teamed up with Olivia Bradley for a double Dutch demonstration," Willa said barely above a whisper. One more word and she'd start crying.

"I'm sorry, Willa," Dad said. "What are you going to do now that Sarah and Lena are out of the picture?"

Willa felt a heavy feeling in her chest, as if she had just swallowed a too-hard piece of bread. Her best friends were never out of the picture. Until now.

"I don't know, Dad," Willa said. She picked up a blank piece of paper and added, "I can't even make a list of ideas—without any ideas."

"Ideas can pop up anywhere, Willa," Dad said.

"Well, they'd better pop soon." Willa sighed.

"Tomorrow is the last day to present ideas to Ms. Denise."

Dad began slicing a yellow pepper as Mom breezed into the kitchen. She quickly placed four narrow cards on the table showing a range of paint colors.

"Those look like cards from a board game, Mom," Willa said.

"They're called paint chips," Mom explained. "I'm trying to decide what colors to have the rooms painted."

"But some of our rooms have wallpaper, Mom," Willa said. "I really like the one with the pink and white roses."

"I know, Willa, but now I'm looking into Danish modern for the inn. Light wood tones, a neutral color palette—"

"Danish?" Dad cut in. "But we live on *Chincoteague Island.*"

Mom pointed to the stove and said, "Just because we don't live in Italy doesn't mean we can't eat spaghetti."

"It's shrimp and linguine," Dad corrected. "But I get your point, Amelia."

Willa popped another raspberry into her mouth. So far Mom had come up with Danish modern, midcentury modern, art deco, and some design style called arts and crafts.

"You have so many ideas, Mom," Willa said. "And I don't have one for my how-to speech."

Mom smiled at Willa. "I'll be making new curtains for the living room to go with the new look. Why not a how-to-make-brand-new-curtains speech?"

Willa appreciated the advice—but she could barely sew on a button.

"Thanks, Mom," Willa answered, "but if I do that—the curtain will probably come down on me."

"By the way, Amelia," Dad said, "Lance Boyd e-mailed his recipe for raspberry torte today."

"That's nice," Mom said over her shoulder as she left the kitchen. "I'll be measuring the windows in the living room if anyone needs me."

Willa's mother didn't seem interested in the recipe, but Willa was. "Where is it, Dad?" she asked, hopping off the stool.

Her father nodded at the sheet of paper near the end of the counter.

Willa picked up the recipe. At the top of

the page was a message from her dad's friend: "Eric, here's my raspberry torte recipe. Happy baking! Lance."

As Willa studied the recipe, her eyes zeroed in on just two words: "How To."

"Oh my gosh," Willa said in almost a whisper. "I can do this. . . . I really think I can do this!"

"What did you say?" Dad asked.

"I just came up with an idea for my how-to speech," Willa exclaimed, waving the recipe through the air. "How to bake a Randy's Razzle-Dazzle Raspberry Torte!"

"The torte?" Dad asked, surprised.

"Ms. Denise wants our how-to speeches to be like getting-to-know-you speeches," Willa explained. "The Family Farm restaurant and Misty Inn are huge parts of me!"

"True," Dad agreed. "But—"

"So Randy's Razzle-Dazzle is much more than a torte, Dad," Willa said. "It's a symbol."

"And I thought it was just a dessert," Dad teased as he lowered the heat on the stove. "I'm also flattered. You know how seriously I take cooking and my restaurant."

Willa nodded. She knew that. It was one of the reasons she admired her father.

"Which is why baking that torte won't be as easy as you think it will be," Dad said, his voice turning serious.

"Why not, Dad? Won't *you* help me?"

"Of course I will," Dad promised. "But you're going to have to earn the recipe by helping out in the kitchen."

"Help out?" Willa asked slowly.

"Most great chefs start out helping other chefs," Dad explained. "Mashing potatoes, slicing vegetables, sometimes even loading the dishwashers."

The thought of all those dirty dishes made Willa wince. But she really wanted to use that recipe. So . . .

"I'll do whatever it takes," she told him.

Willa wiped her raspberry-stained hand, then shook Dad's, relieved she *finally* had a topic for her how-to speech.

"Now don't forget," Dad reminded. "You'll still have your regular chores to do."

Chores! Willa's eyes widened.

"I was so busy thinking about my how-to speech, I forgot to check on Starbuck," Willa said. "What if she's muddy again?"

When Willa found Starbuck, she noticed puddles and patches of mud in the pasture—and a dirty pony. It had rained on and off for the past few days, but why had Starbuck been rolling in the mud for almost a week?

"Have the bugs been bad, girl?" Willa asked gently. "Are you trying to get them off? I wish you could talk, then you could tell me."

Starbuck blinked her chocolate-brown eyes, then flicked her tail to swat a fly away.

"Let's get you cleaned up again, girl," Willa said. She gripped Starbuck's harness and turned her toward the barn.

Starbuck nudged Willa's pocket for more raspberries. Willa didn't have the heart to tell her pony she had eaten all the rest.

"I really think Ms. Denise will like my idea, Starbuck," Willa said. But then she froze with a worried thought. "Unless . . . she doesn't like *raspberries*!"

Chapter 5

"YOU ARE SO LUCKY YOU'RE NOT IN OUR GROUP for the how-to speeches," Sarah whispered over Willa's shoulder.

Willa turned around at her desk. It was Thursday morning. The class hadn't started yet, so there was lots of chatter.

"Why am I lucky?" Willa asked.

"Double Dutch is soooo hard," Sarah groaned,

"even if you're just turning the ropes."

Hard? Willa thought. *Hard is watching your two best friends team up without you.*

But when Willa remembered her raspberry torte, her spirits lifted. "You'll be great, Sarah," Willa told her.

Ms. Denise glanced up from her desk with a smile. "Good morning. I hope everyone is ready to share more ideas for our how-to speeches."

Willa loved the idea of making Randy's Razzle-Dazzle Raspberry Torte but was still worried about Ms. Denise. What if she did hate raspberries? What if—

"We heard some great ideas yesterday," Ms. Denise asked, interrupting Willa's thoughts. "Who would like to go first?"

Willa was ready to raise her hand when

Andrew Dubois shouted, "I have one, Ms. Denise!"

Before Ms. Denise could tell him not to call out, Andrew was already standing, presenting his idea to the class: "I'm really great at throwing darts, so I'd like my speech to be on how to hit a bulls-eye on the dartboard."

Ms. Denise stared at Andrew before asking, "Would you be using real darts?"

"Sure!" Andrew replied. "What other kind are there?"

"In that case, I don't think so, Andrew," Ms. Denise said. "Unless you use magnetic or Velcro darts instead."

"Well, I'll see what I can do," Andrew mumbled as he sat down.

"Next?" Ms. Denise asked.

Willa's hand shot up again. Ms. Denise spotted

Chandra Patel in the back of the room first.

"Yes, Chandra?" Ms. Denise asked.

"Every Saturday morning my mom and I go to Germination and Meditation Farm," Chandra declared.

Willa's eyes widened. Did Chandra just say Germination and Meditation? Was she also planning to bake a pie or torte? Oh no!

"My mom and I go to the farm for yoga classes," Chandra explained. "Which is what I want my how-to speech to be about."

Willa breathed a sigh of relief. Chandra would rather meditate than germinate.

Chandra stood up as she continued. "The poses in Mrs. Beardan's classes are named after fruits and veggies. This one is called the grapevine."

There were a few giggles as Chandra twisted her arms over her head. Ms. Denise smiled approvingly.

"I think yoga is a great idea, Chandra," Ms. Denise said, writing Chandra's idea on the board. "Make sure to bring a mat and wear comfortable clothes."

"I will, Ms. Denise," Chandra said cheerily.

"Any other ideas?" Ms. Denise asked.

Willa *had* to go next. So she jumped up from her seat and blurted, "Speaking of fruit . . ."

"Yes, Willa?" Ms. Denise asked.

"My dad buys produce from Randy Beardan's farm," Willa explained. "He cooks for his restaurant at our bed-and-breakfast, Misty Inn."

Willa stopped to take a breath, then continued, "I have an awesome recipe for Randy's

Razzle-Dazzle Raspberry Torte, and I'd like to show the class how to make it."

Ms. Denise's eyebrows flew up.

Oh no, Willa thought. *She really doesn't like raspberries. . . . I knew it. . . . I knew it—*

"Willa, do you know what my very favorite berry is?" Ms. Denise asked. "Take a wild guess."

"Um . . . raspberries?" Willa asked.

"Yes, raspberries," Ms. Denise confirmed. "Not only are they my favorite fruit, raspberry red is my favorite color."

Willa smiled, her fears drifting away.

"But we don't have an oven in the classroom," Ms. Denise pointed out. "How do you plan to bake your raspberry torte?"

"I figured it out, Ms. Denise," Willa said. "I'll bring in a fresh-out-of-the-oven raspberry torte, which will cool on the windowsill. While that cools, I'll show how to put together the ingredients."

"Then can we eat it?" Dougie Sapperstein asked.

"Sure, you can all have some," Willa said happily.

But when Jasper said, "Ms. Denise, I can't eat Willa's pie; raspberries make me break out in hives," her happiness burst like a bubble.

"*What?*" Willa gasped under her breath.

"Well, Jasper, if raspberries make you break out in hives," Ms. Denise said, "I'm not sure raspberries in the classroom is a good idea after all."

Willa felt like she was the one breaking out in hives. Was her speech about to be rejected?

"Hives?" Dougie scoffed. "Ms. Denise, raspberries make Jasper gag because he doesn't like them. That's all."

"Who asked you?" Jasper snapped.

"Boys," their teacher warned. "Jasper, did you make up the hives story because you don't like raspberries?"

"I guess," Jasper mumbled. "Raspberries look like tiny little brains."

A few giggles. A few "Ewww"s.

"Then you don't have to eat the dessert, Jasper," Ms. Denise said. She turned and wrote Willa's how-to idea on the board: "How to Make a Raspberry Torte."

Willa felt a congratulatory pat on her shoulder from Sarah. She was so excited, she hardly heard Dougie share his idea: how to whistle with a mouth full of cracker crumbs.

"I'm afraid not, Dougie," Ms. Denise said.

Dougie was disappointed, but Willa was over the moon.

On the bus ride home from school, Willa sat next to Chandra Patel. Sarah and Lena sat with Olivia in the back, discussing their next double Dutch practice.

"Aren't Sarah and Lena your best friends?" Chandra asked when she caught Willa glancing back at them. "Don't they want to help you bake your raspberry tart?"

"It's a torte, actually," Willa said with a smile. "And I really don't need anyone to help me."

The bus came to a stop down the hill from Misty Inn. Willa said good-bye to Mr. Carmichael before hurrying ahead of Ben.

"Wait up!" Ben called as Willa raced toward the inn.

"I have to tell Dad about my how-to speech, Ben," Willa called. "Ms. Denise said yes."

Willa neared the kitchen door and noticed a truck parked outside. It was a Germination and Meditation truck.

"Farmer Randy's here," Willa said excitedly as Ben caught up. "I hope he dropped off lots of raspberries so I can practice making the torte."

The kitchen door swung open and out stepped Farmer Randy. He was wearing a denim jacket over his usual faded overalls.

"Guess what, Mr. Beardan?" Willa asked.

"What's that?" Farmer Randy asked. His face was stony, his eyes wide.

"I'm going to be baking a torte for school,"

Willa explained, "using the amazing raspberries from your farm."

"Is that right?" Farmer Randy asked, still not smiling. "I just dropped off a batch of raspberries with your dad."

"Awesome!" Willa said.

Ben brushed past Willa into the kitchen. She remained at the door watching Farmer Randy walk to his truck, still looking unhappy.

As Grandma Edna says, Willa thought, *even horses have good days and bad days.*

She looked at Starbuck grazing in the pasture.

And their muddy days. She sighed to herself. *Not again!*

Chapter 6

"DON'T THEY SELL READY-MADE CRUSTS IN the supermarket?" Ben asked.

"I'll pretend you didn't say that, Ben," Dad said.

It was Saturday morning. Misty Inn was booked with guests there to bird-watch and enjoy the last summer days on Chincoteague

Island. Willa stood next to her father in the kitchen, ready to watch him prepare the torte and see firsthand how it was done.

"Dad likes to make his piecrusts from scratch," she explained to Ben. "Right, Dad?"

"Right," Dad said. "And when you bake *your* torte, so will you."

Taking a break, he wiped his hands on his apron and said, "You know, some restaurants have special pastry chefs."

"How come?" Ben asked.

"Because pastries are as much work as the rest of the meal," Dad explained.

Willa thought making desserts would be easy, but as she gazed at the ingredients on the table—sticks of unsalted butter, vanilla extract, a bag of flour, limes, brown sugar, and of course a glass bowl of fresh raspberries—she realized she had a lot to learn.

"How about some hands-on experience, Willa?" Dad asked. "I can use someone to sprinkle flour on the dough."

"While you get some hands-on experience"—Ben reached toward the raspberry bowl—"I'll get my hands on some berries—"

"Don't even go there," Willa warned.

Ben managed to snatch a few berries before rushing out of the kitchen.

After washing her hands, Willa positioned herself behind the rolled-out dough. She carefully reached into the bag for a pinch of flour.

"Sprinkle it nice and even," Dad directed.

Willa followed her dad's instructions, coughing a bit as flour flew up her nose.

Dad was right, Willa thought, sniffing back a sneeze. *Baking isn't as easy as it looks.*

But almost two hours later, as Dad pulled the warm torte out of the oven, Willa knew her hard work was worth it. The finished product was hot, crispy, and oozing with juicy raspberry goodness.

"Oh, Dad." Willa said as the kitchen filled with the sweet scent of brown sugar and warm raspberries. "It's beautiful!"

"It is," Dad agreed as he placed the torte on the windowsill to cool. "Thanks in part to the world's greatest chef's assistant."

"Thank you!" Willa said, taking a dramatic

bow. "But today was just the dress rehearsal. Next week is the real deal."

"It'll be fine," Dad assured her. He opened the refrigerator and pulled out a carton of heavy cream. "Now, while the pie is cooling, you can prepare the whipped-cream topping."

Willa was about to squeeze some juice for the lime-flavored cream when her mom came into the kitchen.

"Something smells amazing," Mom said. She held up her computer tablet and said, "And speaking of amazing, what do you think?"

Willa studied the photo of a living room, decorated almost entirely in black and white—black furniture, white sofa and chairs, black-and-white rug!

"Um . . . Mom?" Willa asked. "Won't the

guests track mud all over that white carpet?"

"Not unless Starbuck gets in the house!" Mom joked.

Willa heaved a sigh. "I was too busy helping Dad to groom Starbuck today."

"You can groom her after dinner," Mom told Willa. "I'll ask Ben to start setting the tables in the dining room."

Mom looked around and asked, "Where did Ben go, anyway?"

"Maybe he's in the pasture with Starbuck," Willa suggested. She glanced out the kitchen window and gasped. Standing outside on tiptoes was Ben, his hand poised over the windowsill and raspberry torte!

"Ben Dunlap, step away from the raspberry torte now!" Willa shouted.

"A raspberry fell off on the plate," Ben insisted. "I was just going to put it back."

Mom and Dad chuckled as Ben ducked out of sight.

"Now I have two things to worry about." Willa sighed. "Baking a raspberry torte for the class *and* keeping it away from Ben."

Any doubts Willa had about her torte were gone after dessert was served that evening. Willa and Dad watched from the doorway as smiling guests finished every last crumb.

"Randy's Razzle-Dazzle Raspberry Torte is a hit, Dad," Willa whispered excitedly. "A big juicy, creamy hit!"

"It's those smiles and requests for seconds that make me love my work," Dad pointed out dreamily.

"I'll see if we have any more torte left," Willa said, "just in case a guest wants another helping."

When Willa turned back into the kitchen, she gulped. All the ingredients she would need for her how-to speech on Friday reminded her of what a major undertaking this torte was. And how she was making it all by herself.

"All Sarah and Lena have to bring to school," Willa mumbled to herself, "are jump ropes!"

Chapter 7

IT WAS A PEACEFUL SUNDAY MORNING AS WILLA rode Starbuck toward the beach. The summer crowds had left and the boat tours were slowing down. But to Willa, Chincoteague's best-kept secret was the migration of wild birds flying through on their way south.

Willa had already spotted sandpipers, willets, and black skimmers, and hoped to see more birds on the beach that day. She also hoped her arms would stop throbbing.

"Oww," Willa complained, gripping Starbuck's reins. After helping Dad in the kitchen for almost a week, her arms ached from chopping, mixing, and rolling out dough.

Starbuck slowed to a gentle trot along the road.

"Who knew cooking was such hard work?" Willa asked Starbuck. "Not as hard as grooming a pony, but for that I know the drill."

The drill to Willa was knowing that each grooming brush had its own job, starting with the currycomb for tough, deep-set dirt. Once the dirt was brought to the surface, Willa used a brisk brush to dust it off Starbuck's coat. There was a special brush for mane and tail, and a hoof pick to tackle Starbuck's feet. Last but not least came Starbuck's favorite part, a soft clean rag for her face and around her eyes.

That was Willa's recipe for grooming a dirty horse. But the one recipe on her mind that morning was for Randy's Razzle-Dazzle Raspberry Torte.

"Now I need to write the speech," Willa told Starbuck. The only how-to demonstrations Willa had seen were on the shopping network that Dad watched, for the latest cooking gadgets.

"Kids, what do raspberries mean to you?" Willa practiced as she imitated the hosts on TV. "Sticking your tongue out and making funny noises or surprising your tongue with a burst of sweet fruity flavor?"

Starbuck lazily flicked her ears as she continued along the trail.

"Either you're swatting a fly from your ear, Starbuck," Willa giggled, "or you're not too impressed."

As she and her pony rambled on, Willa spotted a surprising flock of snow geese overhead. Those birds usually came through Chincoteague closer to Thanksgiving.

Thanksgiving!

"Maybe I should talk about Thanksgiving," Willa thought out loud. "And how Randy's Razzle-Dazzle Raspberry Torte would make the perfect dessert."

Willa then heaved a big sigh and said, "Or maybe I should just ask Dad to help me write my how-to speech. He's the expert."

They were halfway to the beach when Willa heard a girl singing: "Applesauce, mustard, cider! How many legs has a spider? Two, four—"

The voice seemed to be coming from the Starling house up the road. But it didn't sound like Sarah or her older sister, Katherine—and it certainly wasn't her baby sister, Bess.

Picking up her pace, Starbuck seemed to know she was nearing a familiar place and a friend. Sarah's pony Buttercup had once been housed in the Dunlaps' barn right next to Starbuck.

With a grunt Starbuck came to a stop in front of the Starlings' yard. Willa gulped when she saw Sarah, Lena, and Olivia jumping double Dutch. She hoped they didn't see her, but it was too late. . . .

"Hi, Willa!" Sarah called, smiling at Willa while she turned the ropes. Bad, bad idea!

"Ahhhh!" Olivia cried out as both ropes tangled around her legs.

"Why did you stop turning, Sarah?" Lena called as Olivia stumbled.

"Because Willa's here," Sarah said.

Olivia kicked away the tangled ropes. "You're not supposed to stop for anything," she declared. "Not for a friend, a brother or sister— even a charging bear."

All Willa wanted to do was ride on, but she forced a smile and called, "How's it going?"

"Pretty good," Sarah called back, helping to straighten the ropes. "How's your raspberry pie coming along?"

"Raspberry torte," Willa corrected. "I baked one last night and the guests really liked it."

Olivia cocked her head as she studied

Starbuck. "Is that your pony?" she asked.

"This is Starbuck." Willa nodded. "We were just on our way to the beach."

Lena turned to Sarah and Olivia. "Let's go to the beach too," she said.

"Sounds like a plan!" Sarah said eagerly.

Olivia shook her head. "We can't jump rope on the sand," she said. "Our how-to speech is just four days away so we have to practice until it's perfect."

Sarah and Lena turned disappointed faces toward Willa.

"We'll go another time," Willa promised them. "See you guys in school tomorrow."

She pressed both legs lightly against Starbuck's sides. Her pony shook her mane before trotting onward.

So Olivia wants everything to be perfect, Willa thought as they rode farther away from the house. *Sort of like Dad is when it comes to cooking and baking.*

Starbuck veered onto the path leading to the beach. Willa took in a whiff of clean, salty air. It was then that she made up her mind about her own project.

"Randy's Razzle-Dazzle Raspberry Torte can't just be good anymore," Willa told her pony. "It has to be perfect too."

Chapter 8

"MOM, WHY DO WE HAVE TO SPEND SO MUCH time here?" Willa asked. "It's Wednesday, and I have a ton of stuff to pick up for Friday."

"I know, Willa," Mom said. She was on her knees flipping through a stack of rugs in the home decorating store. "I can't decide between a solid color or floral."

Willa still didn't understand why her

mother wanted to redecorate the inn so soon after they had moved in.

"I thought you loved Misty Inn's old-fashioned style, Mom," Willa said.

"The new style will be old-fashioned," Mom said. "And modern, too."

"Old-fashioned *and* modern?" Willa asked.

Her mother nodded and said, "It's called eclectic."

Willa called it strange. But she wanted to understand her mother's thoughts.

"Mom, why do you want to change everything all of a sudden?" Willa asked.

"I see all the work that goes into Dad's meals," Mom explained with a smile. "It makes me want to do something extra too."

Extra? While Dad cooked, Mom practically ran the whole inn. How would she find extra time to redecorate?

"Maybe I'll fancy up the barn, too," Willa said, tapping her chin thoughtfully. "And trade Starbuck in for a Lipizzaner stallion."

"A Lipizzaner?" Mom asked.

Willa nodded, although deep inside she would never, *ever* trade Starbuck.

"Grandma Edna told me all about Lipizzaners," Willa said. "They're white stallions specially trained to perform fancy moves."

Mom chuckled. "If you think cleaning a muddy butterscotch mare is hard, try cleaning a muddy white one."

Willa frowned at the thought of more mud on Starbuck. It had already rained three days that week.

"I think I'll go with the blue floral rug," Mom decided. "And throw pillows to match."

After a fifteen-minute consultation with the store decorator, Willa and her mom finally left. The rain was just starting again as they rushed into the supermarket.

"Are you sure you know what to buy for your raspberry torte, Willa?" Mom asked.

Willa proudly held up her shopping list. "It's all here, Mom," she said.

"I should have known you made a list," Mom said, smiling. "I'm going to grab a few things for dinner. Can you get started on your own?"

Willa nodded. She looked at her watch and said, "I'll meet you at the ice-cream freezer in twenty minutes."

"Since when is ice cream part of your recipe?" Mom asked.

"It's not," Willa said. "But after I finish this project on Friday, I'm going to need some."

With a smile, Mom walked off. Willa carried a basket down each aisle, selecting ingredients and checking them off her list one by one.

"One carton of heavy cream," Willa said softly, placing the small carton inside her basket. "Shopping for a recipe isn't that hard."

She was about to check the cream off her list when she heard, "Hi, Willa." It was her mom, carrying her basket up the aisle. "I was just on my way to meet you at the ice cream."

Mom nodded at Willa's basket. "I see you got a lot done."

"Shopping is a piece of cake, Mom," Willa said. "Or should I say . . . a piece of torte?"

"I guess making a raspberry torte is more fun than jumping double Dutch, right, honey?" Mom asked.

Willa was about to agree when the word "double" made her gulp.

"Is something wrong?" Mom asked.

"Totally!" Willa groaned. "I forgot I need *two* tortes for my how-to speech. One to make from scratch and one already baked."

"So?" Mom asked.

"So one plus one," Willa said, "equals double of everything I have in this basket."

Willa felt her head begin to spin. Why hadn't she figured it out before she made her list? She was in way over her head.

"Willa, take a deep breath," Mom said gently. "You may have enough there for two tortes—"

"I can't take a chance of falling short," Willa cut in. "Randy's Razzle-Dazzle Raspberry Torte has to be perfect."

Gritting her teeth, Willa turned around. She then retraced her steps, doubling up on every ingredient on her list. By the time she was done, her basket was jam-packed.

"This doesn't even include the bowls and

pans I have to lug to school on Friday." Willa was on the brink of tears.

"It'll be fine," Mom promised. "Just think of all those delicious ripe raspberries Farmer Randy will bring for you tomorrow."

The thought of her raspberries made Willa feel better, but it still wasn't enough.

"I think I'll need that ice cream now, Mom," Willa said. "And make it a double."

Chapter 9

AT SCHOOL THE NEXT MORNING WILLA SAT AT her desk, still tired from shopping and worrying about her how-to speech. But she wasn't the only one. . . .

"I am so nervous, Willa," Sarah whispered while Ms. Denise checked the attendance. "Our double Dutch demo is today."

Willa turned around in her seat. Sarah,

Lena, and Olivia had come to school dressed in the same outfits: red shorts and white T-shirts with the words TEAM SOL printed on the fronts.

"What does SOL stand for?" Willa asked.

"Sarah, Olivia, and Lena," Sarah said. "It also means sun in French."

At eight forty-five on the dot, Ms. Denise stood up from her desk. "Is everybody ready for our first speeches?"

A chorus of yesses filled the classroom.

Ms. Denise looked at the board where she had listed the day's presentations.

"Jasper, you're first today," Ms. Denise announced.

Jasper Langely dragged a small carpet to the front of the classroom. He had told Ms. Denise he would do a how-to speech on getting stains off a rug. What he didn't tell anyone was that the rug would be stained with patches of green goop!

Willa giggled at Ms. Denise's disgusted expression. *I guess Ms. Denise doesn't have any pets!*

Fifteen minutes later Jasper was finishing up. "And remember," he explained as he held up

a spotless rug, "lemon and vinegar is great for getting out icky smells."

"Thank you, Jasper," Ms. Denise said, her nose still wrinkled.

The next student was Piper Chavez. Her speech was on making a pineapple smoothie. Piper remembered all the steps and ingredients. What she forgot was to put the lid on the blender!

The class shrieked as a smoothie geyser gushed all over the table, floor—even on Ms. Denise's red-raspberry-colored patent-leather flats.

"It was an accident, Ms. Denise," Piper wailed.

"While the custodian comes to resolve this," Ms. Denise said, her voice cracking, "we'll go outside to watch Team SOL jump double Dutch."

"Yes," Olivia cheered under her breath.

Willa turned to wish Sarah luck. But Team SOL was already racing out the door with their jump ropes.

They're excited, but so am I, Willa thought as she followed her class to the school yard. *I'm getting my raspberry delivery this afternoon!*

Once outside, Ms. Denise's class formed a semicircle around Sarah, Lena, and Olivia.

"Okay, Team SOL," Ms. Denise said with a smile. "Whenever you're ready, please start your introduction."

Olivia cleared her throat. She then threw back her head and said with a loud, clear voice:

"Double Dutch might sound like a yummy hot chocolate drink, but did you know it's a way to jump rope with two ropes?"

Willa noticed Olivia's sneaker laces had red pom-poms at the ends. Cool.

"It's an old way to jump rope too," Sarah chimed in. "The game started in ancient Egypt and China. Dutch kids played the game in old New Amsterdam. That's what New York used to be called."

"And speaking of big cities," Lena piped up. "Double Dutch is super popular with city kids."

"So what are we waiting for Team SOL?" Olivia declared, lifting a rope in each hand. "Let's hop to it!"

Sarah and Lena took hold of the rope

handles. After a nod from Olivia, they turned both ropes in opposite directions as they began to sing: "Red hot pepper in a pot! Who's got more than our team's got? Ten, twenty, forty—"

Holding her head high, Olivia high-stepped over the spinning ropes. Sarah and Lena turned the ropes in perfect rhythm too, singing: "Dancer, dancer, turn around. Dancer, dancer, touch the ground!"

Still jumping, Olivia began to spin. But before

she could spin all the way around, a tangled jump rope sent her spilling to the ground.

"Owwww!" Olivia cried, her hand clutching her ankle. Her foot was still tangled within the snarled jump rope.

Concerned, Willa and her classmates stepped forward. Ms. Denise kneeled down next to Olivia, a hand on her shoulder.

"Olivia, are you all right?" Ms. Denise asked.

"I think I twisted my ankle," Olivia wailed. "One of my pom-poms got stuck in the ropes. What was I thinking wearing those today?"

Ms. Denise asked Chandra to go for the school nurse. She then turned back to Olivia and said gently, "It's okay, Olivia. Team SOL's how-to speech was very good. As for the jumping, not everything has to be perfect—"

"Yes, it does, Ms. Denise," Olivia said, her tear-filled eyes wide, "at least when it comes to double Dutch."

When the nurse arrived, Ms. Denise's class filed back into school. Sarah and Lena looked miserable as they dragged the jump ropes behind them.

"Sorry that happened," Willa told them.

"We're sorry too," Lena groaned. "I don't want to see another jump rope until I'm in college."

"You're so lucky you're baking a pie, Willa," Sarah said. "What could go wrong with raspberries?"

"It's a torte," Willa said, for what seemed like the fiftieth time.

"What's the difference?" Lena asked.

Willa flashed a smile and said, "Wait until tomorrow and you'll see!"

Chapter 10

"HOW WERE THE SPEECHES TODAY, WILLA?" Ben asked after he and Willa stepped off the bus.

"Some were boring," Willa said. She then thought of the smoothie and double Dutch disasters and frowned. "Others were not so boring."

When Ben stopped to say hi to New Cat, Willa spotted the Germination and Meditation truck.

"My raspberries!" Willa sang as she hurried

up the driveway. The kitchen door opened and out stepped Farmer Randy, looking as glum as could be.

"Hi, Farmer Randy!" Willa called. "Did you bring the raspberries for my assignment?"

The farmer shook his head slightly as he continued toward his truck. "Rain," he mumbled. "Lots of rain this week."

Puzzled, Willa watched Farmer Randy climb into his truck. Why did he shake his head? And why the weather report? Everyone knew it had rained practically all week.

As long as my raspberries are bright, red, and juicy, Willa thought as she opened the kitchen door, *who cares if we have another week of rain?*

Willa stepped into the kitchen. She didn't see Dad or Mom. Instead, she saw the broccoli, carrots, apples, and plums that Farmer Randy had dropped off. But where were the raspberries?

Probably in the refrigerator, Willa thought.

Willa felt a cold blast as she swung open the refrigerator door. She looked from shelf to shelf and through the crisper bin. She found all kinds of foods, but not one single raspberry.

Just then Willa's father came into the kitchen. "Hi, honey," he said.

Shutting the refrigerator door, Willa spun around. "Where are my raspberries, Dad?"

Her father didn't answer. Instead, he wrapped his arms around Willa and gave her a hug. Willa knew something was wrong.

"Farmer Randy just broke the news," Dad said. "All the rain we've had caused mold to grow on the raspberry plants."

Willa stared up at her dad. "What does that mean? I won't have any raspberries for my torte?" she asked, her voice cracked.

"No, honey," Dad said. "I'm sorry."

Willa bit her lip to keep from crying. Now she knew how Olivia felt when she fell during double Dutch. Miserable!

"What am I going to do, Dad?" Willa asked. "I bought all the ingredients—times two. And my demonstration is tomorrow."

"Randy dropped off a basket of apples for you, free of charge," Mom said, coming into the kitchen. "Maybe you can bake a yummy apple torte for the class."

Willa stared at her parents. Apples? What were they talking about? There was *no* way she could learn how to thinly slice apples, not to mention arranging them perfectly, in one evening.

"Should we come up with a fabulous apple torte recipe?" Dad asked. "What says fall more than apples?"

Willa was too upset to think of or consider other recipes. She needed to leave the kitchen fast.

"I'm going to check on Starbuck now," Willa said. "Can we talk about my speech after I get back?"

"Of course, Willa," Dad said.

"Whenever you're ready," Mom added.

Once outside, Willa walked straight past Ben to the pasture where Starbuck was. As if things couldn't get worse, her pony was covered head to tail with mud again.

"Lots of rain makes lots of mud," Willa sighed, "and no raspberries."

Willa led Starbuck back to the barn. Once she was in her stall, Willa began grabbing the grooming brushes one by one.

"I may not know how to bake an apple torte," Willa told Starbuck, "but at least I know how to clean mud off a pony."

Willa was about to grab the mane-and-tail brush when her hand froze in the air.

Clean . . . mud . . . pony?

Suddenly everything clicked. She didn't *have* to bake a raspberry torte or an apple torte, either. She had a new how-to idea that would tell the class something important about her. *Super important!*

"Oh my gosh, Starbuck, that's it!" Willa exclaimed. "I'm going to show the class how to clean a dirty pony!"

Chapter 11

"BEN, ARE YOU DOING YOGA?" WILLA ASKED. "You look like one of those twisted straws!"

Ben sat cross-legged on the floor in Willa's room, his arms crossed too.

"You had your fingers crossed that you'll be able to bring Starbuck to school tomorrow," Ben explained, "so I'm crossing everything for you—even my eyes!"

Willa giggled as Ben crossed his eyes. But as she petted New Cat, who was curled up on her bed, she felt butterflies flutter inside her stomach. Mom was on the phone with Ms. Denise. What would her teacher say about Starbuck?

Fortunately, Willa didn't have to wait long for an answer.

"Your new speech has been approved!" her mother announced.

"Woo-hoo!" Willa cheered. She jumped off the bed, bouncing off New Cat. "What did Ms. Denise say? Does she like ponies?"

"At first she was nervous," Mom admitted. "If Olivia could get hurt jumping rope, a horse on the school grounds seemed like asking for trouble."

When Willa looked worried, Mom continued.

"But I told Ms. Denise how ponies were second nature for you. I also told her that Starbuck was a mare beyond compare . . . even when muddy."

"Thanks, Mom," Willa said. She turned to her brother, still twisted on the floor. "You can untangle yourself now, Ben."

"It worked!" Ben said, grinning.

Mom smiled at Ben, then Willa. "I'm proud of you, honey, for thinking of a new how-to speech so quickly."

"I should have thought of that idea in the first place," Willa said. "The Family Farm is a big part of my life, but Starbuck is even bigger."

Willa shrugged her shoulders. "It's also a natural choice for me. It makes sense to be myself and not to be too fussy and fancy just to impress the class."

"Excellent advice," Mom declared.

"*Advice?*" Willa asked.

"All that redecorating made me much too nervous and stressed," Mom explained. "I don't know why I wanted Misty Inn to be something it isn't."

"You mean no more trips to the design store?" Willa asked excitedly. "Or Danish modern? Or shabby chic?"

"More like Chincoteague comfy." Mom smiled. "And all pets will be welcome inside the house . . . with the exception of horses, of course."

"Hear that, New Cat?" Ben asked.

"Sounds good to me," Willa declared with a smile. Because for the first time in days, she had a lot to smile about!

♥

"Ponies can be fun," Willa told her class the next morning in a field behind the school. "But as you can see, they can also be a little messy—especially when they roll in the mud."

As she made her introduction, Willa turned toward a dirt-encrusted Starbuck. A few feet away stood Mom, who had brought Starbuck to school that morning.

Everyone in Willa's class, even Ms. Denise, smiled at Starbuck. Everyone except Olivia, who had stayed home to rest her sprained ankle.

"Grooming a muddy mare doesn't have to be a nightmare," Willa said, hoping they got her joke, "as long as you have the right tools."

Willa swept her hand over the grooming brushes lined neatly on a blanket on the ground.

"Now that we have the tools, here are the rules."

While Willa described each brush, Starbuck stood at attention as if she knew she was the star of the speech.

Others in the class also had ponies, but they seemed to enjoy watching and hearing about something they already knew.

"It's important to gently run your hand along your horse's side so she knows where you are," Willa said, and demonstrated. "And, most important, so she doesn't become surprised. A surprised pony can be a skittish pony."

Willa picked up the first brush. After a

quick demonstration on its use, she said, "Would someone like to try using the currycomb? The currycomb brushes out deep-set dirt."

Most hands went up. Willa smiled at Sarah and said, "Sarah has a pony. Maybe she'd like to show how it's done."

Sarah smiled too as she took the brush from Willa. Starbuck snorted softly as Sarah brushed her side with a circular motion. After Sarah finished a section of her coat, Willa held up the next grooming tool, the brisk brush.

"When dirt is loose, it's important to dust it off like this," Willa said as she flicked the brush lightly over Starbuck's shoulder. "Who wants to try the brisk brush?"

Lena's hand shot up first. "Lena, go for it," Willa said with a grin.

While Lena gently used the brisk brush, Sarah groomed Starbuck's other side. At the same time Willa demonstrated the mane-and-tail brush.

"As you can all see," Willa told the class after they finished, "a clean horse is a happy horse."

Starbuck bobbed her head, which made everyone laugh—especially Ms. Denise.

"Does anyone have questions for Willa?" Ms. Denise asked. Almost all hands went up.

"Is it true Starbuck is a real Chincoteague pony?"

"Why do ponies roll in the mud?"

"Does Starbuck ever give you a hard time when you're trying to clean her?"

Willa answered each question as best she could until Ms. Denise said, "Thank you, Willa. That was an excellent how-to speech."

"Thanks, Ms. Denise," Willa said. She couldn't believe how happy and accomplished she felt.

Mom gave Willa a thumbs-up. She then took hold of Starbuck's reins and led her out of the school yard. While the kids watched the buckskin Chincoteague leave, Sarah and Lena walked over to Willa.

"That was awesome, Willa," Sarah said.

"Better than our how-to speech," Lena said. "Too bad Olivia had to miss this."

"I have an idea," Willa said. "Why don't we visit Olivia tomorrow? Maybe I'll bake a get-well apple pie."

"Don't you mean apple torte?" Sarah asked.

Willa shook her head. "I'm keeping things simple," she said, "at least for now."

As the girls walked together to their classroom, Willa was over-the-moon happy. Not only was her how-to speech a success, she finally did get to team up with her three best friends: Sarah, Lena—and Starbuck!

ACKNOWLEDGMENTS

Thanks to the entire Aladdin team for bringing this book to life. Karen Nagel's enthusiasm and humor make any project a pleasure. Thanks to her and to Fiona Simpson for trusting this lifelong city girl to imagine life on Chincoteague Island. Much thanks to Kristin Earhart for her wonderful vision of Misty Inn and its characters. Her knowledge and love of horses were incredibly helpful and inspiring. Thanks also to Serena Geddes, whose illustrations bring so much sparkle to the series, and to Laura Lyn DiSiena, for beautifully designing the series. Last but not least, a huge thanks to my family and forever friends—you're always there to lend support and an occasional ear for my ideas, day or night.

Saddle up for a new world of classic horse tales!

For a full round-up of pony stories inspired by Marguerite Henry's *Misty of Chincoteague* visit **PoniesOfChincoteague.com**!

Simon & Schuster Children's Publishing · **A CBS COMPANY**

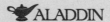